MW01048884

Curiosity of a Clownfish

Photography by Steve Parish
Text by Kylie Currey

Steve Parish™

KIDS

www.steveparish.com.au

The shallow waters of the coral reef are warm and calm. The stinging tentacles of purple anemones sway in the currents, but the white stripe clownfish family live happily among the tentacles without being stung.

Here, in their anemone home, they are safe from predators and, in return, they fight off other fish that eat anemones. Life under water is great!

Until… a massive storm begins to brew. The winds begin to blow. The waves begin to crash.

The clownfish are rumbled and tumbled in all directions, far away from their anemone home.

One little clownfish finds himself all alone in a deep, dark ocean world. Down here, fish find protection in numbers. They swim by slowly, always on the lookout for predators.

Although he is not in danger from these fish, White Stripe knows he must find his anemone home soon!

Around the corner, he sees an incredible sight – small, striped cleaner wrasses dance fearlessly in and out of the gaping mouths of two huge fish! White Stripe notices that by pecking off the tiny animals living around

the fishes' mouths and gills, the little fish are not only helping the big fish, they're grabbing an easy meal for themselves.

Continuing on his way, White Stripe comes face-to-face with another clownfish! She is from the blue stripe family, and she's also in search of her anemone home.

The wrasses have followed. They begin to peck at the slimy scales of the clownfish. Oooh…that tickles! The clownfish swim away quickly, off to find their homes.

Heading into shallower waters, the two clownfish encounter the biggest, hugest fish they've ever seen!

Called Potato Cod, these slow-moving, gentle giants love to be pecked and tickled around their big, thick lips by the cleaner wrasse.

As they swim through the branching coral, the clownfish meet other colourful reef fish. Two yellow and blue angelfish swim in close for a friendly peek.

A harlequin tuskfish, with bright orange stripes, swims overhead. The graceful lionfish, with its prickly, poisonous spines, is just as curious and comes closer for a look at the two clownfish.

On their journey, the clownfish meet two other fish that are almost the same size as they are. The bright yellow boxfish and the spiny cowfish were also washed away by the storm.

For a while, the four little fish enjoy swimming together, but soon it will be night time and they still need to reach the safety of their homes.

It's getting dark and the clownfish must watch out for predators lurking beneath the coral. They spy some strange, fishy behaviour. Why is a long, thin trumpetfish swimming with a group of Moses perch?

Aha! Using its colour as camouflage, the trumpetfish becomes a sneaky predator. It creeps up close to its prey and sucks it in through its long, tube-like snout.

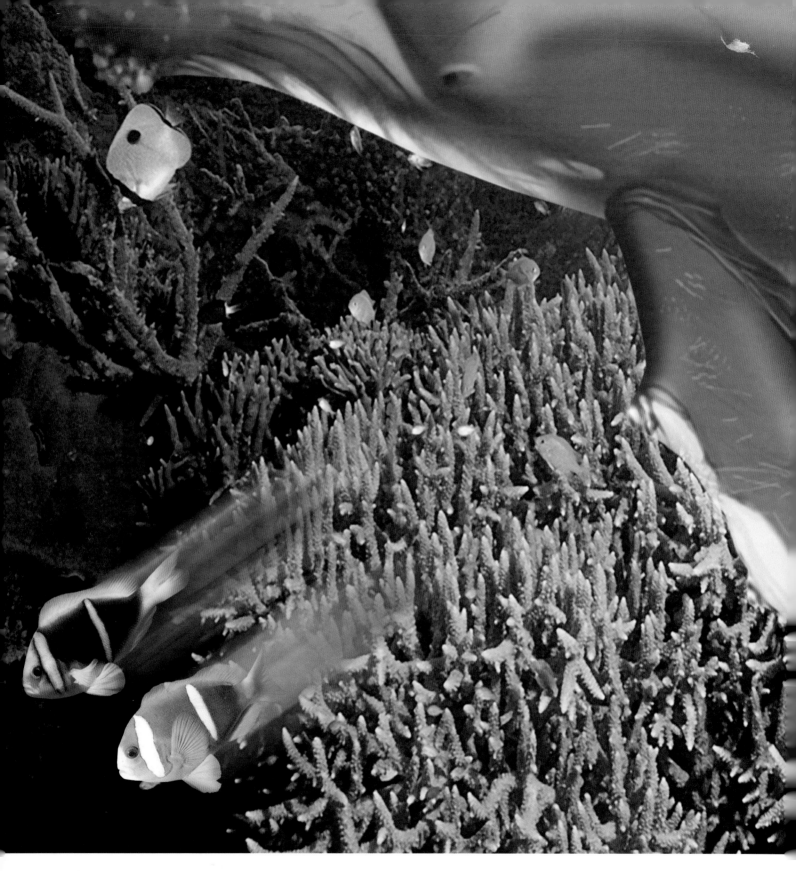

All of a sudden, the moonlight disappears and the little clownfish are plunged into darkness. A huge WHOOSH of water from above forces White Stripe and Blue Stripe down towards the sea bed.

They look back to see an enormous humpback whale and her calf
swimming above them…WHOOSH!

White Stripe and Blue Stripe take shelter in a cave beneath the coral.
Beams of red light sweep over them and shine on the sand below.
Above them swims a school of pineapple fish.

Each fish has a glowing piece of skin at the side of its mouth. Pineapple fish use this light to scan the sea bed in search of tiny shrimps to eat.

At first light, White Stripe and Blue Stripe set off again in search of their homes. Towards the surface, large schools of predatory fish flash by at high speed.

Four large kingfish chase close behind a school of shimmering trevally. The little clownfish know that if they don't move right now, they might become food for these hunters!

Uh-oh! Stay very still little clownfish. Two blacktip sharks are scanning the reef for schools of fish to hunt. The approaching sharks slow down. They sense vibrations.

White Stripe and Blue Stripe begin to quiver in fear, but, fortunately, the sharks swim overhead in the direction of the kingfish and trevally. Phew!

As the clownfish enter the shallows, two playful bottlenose dolphins swim in to greet them. White Stripe and Blue Stripe recognise the dolphins' friendly faces.

They begin to wiggle their tails and swim faster, excited that their anemone homes are close. Soon they will be safe!

Finally… they are home at last! Blue Stripe darts off to her family. The white stripe family all flicker their tails, flap their fins and dart in and out of their anemone home. They are so happy that White Stripe is back.

White Stripe is also very happy to be home. As he swims through his anemone, the soft, finger-like tentacles tickle his scales. Oooh...that's a nice tickle!

Learn About Clownfish...

Clownfish are also called *anemonefish* because they live in large sea anemones.

Many different types, or *species*, of clownfish live on the reef and each species has a favourite type of anemone in which it lives.

barrier reef anemonefish

tomato anemonefish

Clownfish look after their anemone homes by fighting off other fish, like the long-nosed butterflyfish, which nibble at the ends of anemone tentacles.

long-nosed butterflyfish

Anemones have stinging tentacles that stop some fish from eating them and others from living in them. But clownfish are covered in a slimy coating called *mucous*, which protects them from the anemone's sting. Inside the anemone, a clownfish is safe from predators.

black anemonefish

Female clownfish are larger than males. Incredibly, if the female dies, the male changes into a female so that it can lay eggs! The stinging tentacles of the anemone help protect the eggs. They stop other fish, which may eat the eggs before they hatch, from getting too close.

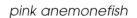

pink anemonefish